Owlet

the great horned owl

Also by
IRENE BRADY
America's Horses and Ponies
A Mouse Named Mus

Written and illustrated by Irene Brady

Owlet
the
great
horned
owl

Houghton Mifflin Company

Boston 1974

For Dr. Walsh and
the Oregon School of Art

And for Laura

Library of Congress Cataloging in Publication Data

Brady, Irene
  Owlet.

  SUMMARY: Chronicles the life of a great horned
owl from the time he is hatched until he mates and
begins his own family.

  1. Horned owl--Juvenile literature. (1. horned
owl. 2. Owls) I. Title.
QL696.S83B7   598.9'7   74-5483
ISBN 0-395-18519-X

Owlet
the great horned owl

ONE SHIVERY WINTER MORNING in the dark pine woods, a shadow flew silently through the trees and lit on a messy pile of sticks and twigs high in a tall pine. The shadow was Mother Great Horned Owl coming home from hunting to the nest to do something very important. It was time to lay the egg.

She stepped into the middle of the creaky nest and turned around once, twice, three times. Then she sat very still, and in a minute there was a soft *plop* as a roundish white egg dropped into the nest. Feeling carefully with her furry toes, she rolled the egg under her fluffy breast feathers to keep it warm.

As Mother Owl began her long wait for the egg to hatch, big white snowflakes started to fall. Soon she was covered with a soft white blanket. She blinked and snuggled down into the nest to keep warm. She couldn't leave her egg now or it would freeze.

Through the snowy woods she saw a dark shape drifting toward her. It was her mate coming to see where she was. He spread his huge wings as he got close to the nest and landed lightly on the edge.

"Whoooo!" he cried. As soon as he saw that she was brooding an egg in the nest, all covered with snow, he knew what had happened. He leaped off the nest, strongly beating his softly feathered wings, and drifted off into the snowstorm to try to find her something to nibble.

The mother owl sat on the nest and brooded her egg for thirty-three wintry days and nights, as all mother Great Horned Owls do. She turned the egg over frequently with her feet and beak so its bottom side wouldn't get cold. The days were icy and she often shivered, but she didn't ever leave the nest for more than two or three minutes at a time. Her mate hunted all the long hours of the nights to find enough food to feed them both. Owls do most of their hunting at night. In the daytime the songbirds often chase them with noisy cries, perhaps to warn others that an

enemy is nearby. With all that noise going on, owls can't catch *anything*. So they hunt at night when songbirds are asleep. During the thirty-three days of brooding, the male owl watched over the mother owl and her egg from his roost tree nearby.

On the morning of the thirty-third day the owlet inside the egg started pipping. First there was a long crack from one side of the egg to the other. Then the edges of the crack were chipped away from inside the egg and a hole appeared. There, inside, was Owlet's little wet head! His beak with its tough egg tooth on the tip pecked at the hard shell. In a few days the egg tooth would fall off, but just now Owlet needed it to chip his way out of the shell.

Mother Owl peered at her egg with big eyes. This was her very first egg. She hopped up and down in the nest hooting, "Kwa-kwa-hooo!" It's a wonder she didn't squash Owlet quite flat inside his eggshell! Her mate came over to the nest from his roost tree to see what all the excitement was about. When he saw Owlet popping out of his egg he hooted, "Hu-hu-hu-hu-hu!" very loud and fast. Then he flew into the woods to find food for his family, even though it *was* in the middle of the day!

By the time Owlet had struggled out of his damp shell and cuddled under his mother's warm breast, his father had brought two sparrows, seven meadow mice, half a rabbit (he had eaten

the other half), and a skunk, and he piled them all around the edge of the nest.

His mother ate part of the rabbit and pulled it down into the nest to tear off tiny bite-sized pieces for Owlet, but he was too tired from hatching to eat a thing. Besides, he wasn't even dry yet. So he shivered and snuggled under Mother, his downy white feathers slowly fluffing up as they dried.

Owlet wasn't very pretty. He was about as big as a potato, with a big head and a long heavy beak. His neck was so skinny and weak that it couldn't even hold up his head. His eyes wouldn't open for about another week.

He peeped happily when he got dry and warm, and after a while he tried a little bit of rabbit supper. Around him on the edge of the nest the meadow mice and sparrows and skunk froze solid. But, as his first day ended, Owlet was warm under Mother Owl.

Owlet's mother sat on him most of the time. Sometimes she backed up to the edge of the nest to get rid of droppings, and sometimes she leaned frontward over the side of the nest to burp up pellets.

When an owl eats its prey, the meat, fat, and skin go into the

the owl's stomach as nourishment. But bones, fur, and feathers, which an owl can't digest, are pressed into tight wads a little bigger than a man's thumb — pellets — which the owl belches up several hours later.

Sometimes Owlet peeped noisily when his mother let the cold air rush in. Then she would hop back into the nest and settle down over him hissing, and he would be quiet.

Owlet grew fast. When he was five days old he was all bristly with pinfeathers, and he was *really* ugly. When he was nine days old, his eyes started to open. Mostly all he saw were his mother's breast feathers, but sometimes he got a blurry look at the

sides of the nest, a rabbit's foot, or a branch that hung over the nest. Once he saw his father pop out of the gloom with a mouse hanging from his beak. Owlet's yellow-brown eyes stared up in alarm at the feathery horns, huge, saucer-round eyes, and fierce beak! Then he squeaked with fright and scrambled back under his mother, holding tightly to her toes until he stopped shivering.

When Owlet was two weeks old he was almost as big as a pigeon. His body pinfeathers had turned to grayish-tan fluff, and he snapped and clicked his beak the way he heard his parents do when his father brought food to the nest.

Owlet snapped and clicked at everything. He snapped at his

mother's talons when she stepped on him. He clicked at a wiggly stick in the nest. And sometimes he snapped at his father when the old owl landed at the nest with something to eat.

The baby owl wasn't a ball of white fluff anymore. His back was now speckled with brown feathers. His wings and tail had big, tough pinfeathers bursting from the edges and tips. Soon he'd have wing feathers and tail feathers.

The nest in the tall pine wasn't very big or strong. It's a good thing his mother hadn't laid two or three, or even four or five eggs, as Great Horned Owls often do. There just wasn't enough room. The nest had been built long ago by red-tailed hawks and over the years many of the sticks had fallen out. Great Horned Owls don't ever build or patch their own nests. They always borrow or steal nests from other birds or squirrels, or use hollow trees. This nest was just about used up.

On Owlet's third-week birthday, he was half as big as his parents. His mother couldn't keep all of him tucked under her warm feathers. First his tail would get goosebumps, then his left wing, then his head. Nothing seemed to fit anymore. But things usually work out just right when nature is left to itself. Just as Owlet got too big to fit under his mother, spring came and the weather got warm and sunny.

Siskiyou County

As Owlet got bigger and hungrier, his mother began to leave the nest to hunt the woods and meadows for more food. She sometimes brought back strange things like frogs and snakes. Once she brought a catfish!

Both his parents were gone one night when there was a scratching and scrabbling at the bottom of the tree. As the scratching sounds got closer and louder, Owlet's feathers stood out stiffer and straighter from his body until he looked almost as big as his father. His round eyes got even rounder. He started to hiss with fright and clack his beak as loud as he could.

Suddenly a hungry raccoon lurched up over the nest's edge!

But he got a surprise! Instead of finding a helpless baby bird, he found Owlet, who lurched over onto his feathery back and snatched and grabbed at the raccoon's face with his talons!

With an astonished snort, the raccoon slipped and fell down to a lower branch just as Owlet's mother and father returned together from hunting. Father's beak was full of squirrel, but he dropped it in a flash and dived at the frightened raccoon with a fierce scream. WHACK! Father hit him a mighty blow on one side with his talons and wings. WHAM! Mother knocked him right off the branch. The raccoon fell out of the tree with a loud crash and a squeal. Then he crept off under some bushes where the owls couldn't attack him.

As his mother lit on the nest, Owlet snapped and clicked excitedly until she hissed softly and covered him with her wing like a blanket. She didn't leave him again that night.

Owlet was growing up. For quite a while he had been backing to the edge of the nest to make droppings. Many owlets lose their grip at the edge and fall out of the nest when they are first learning to do this. One day Owlet *almost* fell off backward, but he was quick and strong. With his beak he grabbed a stick that poked out of the nest, and, using both his wings and feet, he pulled himself back up to the top. He was much more careful after that!

By now he was beginning to look more like a Great Horned Owl. His ear tufts — which give the Great Horned Owl its name — were starting to poke up on the top of his head. His eyes were light yellow and his wing feathers were getting longer and stronger. Now that he was four weeks old, he could puff out his feathers until he was the size of a football.

Owlet was hungry all the time. When he was hungry, he screeched. Sometimes his mother and father had to hunt during the day to keep him quiet. The best way to shut him up was to poke a leg of muskrat or pheasant into his open mouth.

Owlet's parents didn't like to hunt in the daytime. His mother would rather sit on the nest and nap. His father would rather stand tall and narrow in the leafy roost tree or in a thicket overgrown with vines and nap. After all, they'd been working hard all night. If his father stood very close to the tree trunk, he was almost invisible. But if he roosted farther out on the limb, a songbird or crow might see him. Then he would be attacked by a crowd of screaming birds flying at his head and sometimes even pecking him as they dived. He always tried to ignore those noisy birds, but they usually tormented him until he would have to fly away to find a more secret place to sleep.

One night, when Owlet was about five weeks old, he suddenly knew it was time to leave the nest. Only an owlet knows what it is that makes an owlet decide it's time to go see the world. He stood up in the nest and fluffed his feathers and snapped his beak uneasily. Then he jumped up on the edge of the nest and looked down at the ground. He peered up at the starry sky. He looked through the trees all around. Then, almost before he knew what he was doing, he jumped and went sailing through the air at a terrific speed straight toward the ground. He frantically stuck his wings out on each side and the air whizzed past a little slower. A second later he landed with a hard *thump* on the forest

floor, sending pine cones rattling and rolling in all directions.

Whoosh! All the air went out of him. When he got his breath back he looked around in fright. Next to him was a leaning tree, and the same urge that had made him jump out of the nest sent him clawing and scratching his way up the leaning trunk until he was perching on a limb about ten feet above the ground.

Owlet looked around with big yellow eyes. Everything looked different from his new roost, but one thing was still the same: he was hungry. He opened his beak wide and squawked his "hungry" squawk.

A few minutes later a dark shadow passed overhead. Owlet's eyes couldn't see very well yet because he was so young, but that shadow looked like somebody with some food, so he squawked again. There was a confused hoot as his mother tried to find him in the nest. Then she jumped off the nest to look for little Owlet. When he screeched again she found him and came to him with the mouse she had been carrying. He clutched it in one taloned foot and ate it headfirst like a candy bar, which is the best way to eat a mouse.

In the weeks that followed, Owlet's parents had to look all over the woods for him as he hopped from limb to stump to bush in his exploring. But it wasn't hard to find him because he made the woods ring with hungry screeches and squawks.

It was the middle of April now, and Owlet, like all young Great Horned Owls, was learning a good deal about the forest around him. One of the first things he learned was where *not* to perch. As his wing feathers grew out and his wings got stronger, Owlet began making short, gliding, almost-flying leaps from tree to tree. At the end of his first glide he landed on a little twig that wasn't strong enough to hold him. Down it drooped, with Owlet tightly clutching it, until he was hanging upside down in midair! He flapped his half-grown wings and screeched until he was so tired that his feet slipped off the twig and he crashed to the

ground. The very same thing happened three times in a row before Owlet finally learned his lesson. After that he chose stronger branches to land on.

By the time Owlet was eight weeks old, his feathers were becoming beautifully marked with dark bars just like his parents'. The fluffy feathers on his breast were two inches deep and he was just about as big as his parents were. By now, his wings had all their feathers. Owlet could flap for quite a distance through the woods before he had to stop and rest. But his father and mother still had to feed him.

That wasn't Owlet's fault, really. Like all Great Horned Owlets, he *tried* to catch things all the time. He'd hear a small creature in the dry leaves or maybe even see it, and he'd dive right down to it. But when he got there he just didn't know what to do. Time after time he'd land next to a mouse or beetle, lean toward it, and open his mouth wide. But none of them were kind enough to jump in. In fact, most of them ran the other direction. One day, a big juicy June beetle tried to run up Owlet's leg to hide, and Owlet grabbed it and swallowed it almost before he knew what had happened. It wasn't long before Owlet learned to catch his beetles by pecking or grabbing them with his talons. Mice were still too quick for him to catch, but a few days later Owlet caught his first bird.

Even a young owl can fly silently because its feathers are velvety with soft edges, just like the feathers of grown-up owls. Owlet saw the sparrow and dived down to it, landing almost on top of it. The sparrow had no room to fly and Owlet grabbed it and killed it instantly. What a feast! Before he ate it, he pulled off most of the feathers, as owls usually do. When he was finished he strutted around the pile of feathers for a few minutes, puffing out his feathers and clacking his beak before flying away. But the beetles and the bird were only good-luck catches, and Owlet still had to screech and beg for food from his parents.

During the first part of the summer, Owlet did most of his hunting in the daytime. As long as his feathers were fuzzy and pale, the songbirds and crows didn't bother him. But Owlet had other enemies besides the birds, and one day he met one bigger than himself.

On that day a coyote was passing nearby and he heard Owlet screeching for food from a low stump. The coyote was only a yearling born last spring. If he had known anything about baby Great Horned Owls, he would have kept right on going down the trail. But he had never tried to catch one before and this noisy bird hidden behind the currant bushes sounded good enough to

eat. The coyote made a big circle so he could sneak up behind Owlet. Little Owlet couldn't see the coyote, but owls have good ears, and Owlet could hear every step the coyote took. As the coyote circled around behind Owlet, Owlet's head turned farther and farther around to face his enemy. His screeching stopped and his eyes got big and round. Suddenly the footsteps started to come closer, and Owlet quickly turned to face the danger. He spread out his wings and feathers until he looked as big as a bushel basket.

By the time the coyote's wet black nose and keen gray eyes finally poked through the leaves of the currant bush, Owlet was a real monster. The coyote froze in his tracks, and as he did Owlet

gave a terrible hiss and scream. He snapped his beak ferociously, threw himself back on his tail feathers, and spread out his talons like razor-sharp hooks!

"Yowp!" yelped the coyote, when he saw the monster on the stump. With his ears flat against his head and his tail between his legs, he scrambled for the protection of the bushes and the dark woods.

Hissing and snapping, Owlet hopped to his feet and crouched warily. Little by little his feathers began to flatten until Owlet looked like an owl again. Off through the woods the sounds of the fleeing coyote got fainter and fainter, until they completely died away. Owlet snapped his beak toward the vanished coyote as a final warning, then he began to screech once more for food as if nothing had happened at all.

By the end of the summer, Owlet had most of his grown-up feathers. He looked as big and as old as his mother and father except for a few leftover downy feathers poking out here and there. Since he had grown his adult feathers, the crows had mobbed him several times when he was hunting and exploring in the daytime. They seemed to sense that he had become more dangerous now that he wasn't covered with light-colored down. Two crows attacked him one day as he flew across a meadow, and

Owlet, helpless to fight back in midair, left behind him a trail of falling feathers. He suffered from cuts and bruises from their sharp beaks for several days, and then began to sit quietly in leafy trees until the sun went down.

An owl has better eyes than people do. In the daytime owls can see about as well as people can, but at night they can see much better than any human. A black cloudy night only seems as dark as a cloudy afternoon to an owl.

To Owlet it didn't make much difference whether he hunted day or night because he hardly ever caught anything anyway.

Here he was, a full-sized owl in grown-up feathers, screeching baby screeches and begging his parents for food!

He was very hungry one evening and he decided to find his parents and scream at them. He glided silently among the trees, watching for his parents and clacking his beak angrily. A snapping twig and slight movement ahead suddenly excited him. Ah! Perhaps he would be quick enough to grab *this* one before it ran away! He dived without a sound with his talons stretched out to land on the ground beside his prey. But, instead of landing on cool flat ground, his feet landed on warm wiggly mouse! He

hissed and squeezed his sharp talons in surprise and then he was sprawling on the ground with the mouse clutched in his toes! Owlet's big golden eyes widened and blinked as he stared at the mouse, then he opened his beak and ate it hungrily.

He heard two more rustles in the dry leaves that night. And even though he tried to land on them in the new way, he missed them both. He came a lot closer to catching the second one, though, than the first.

After that, in the rustling dry-leaf autumn woods, Owlet tried very hard to catch his own food. By the time the winter snows began to blanket the bare trees, he was catching almost enough to feed himself. As the days got colder, Owlet wandered farther and farther looking for his own food. If he didn't find enough to eat, his parents were always somewhere nearby with a piece of rabbit or maybe a chickadee to help him out.

One snowy morning just before dawn, when Owlet was still hungry, he flew screeching through the woods to beg some food from his parents. But the woods looked strange; he had wandered a long way looking for food. He called and called, straining to hear an answering hoot or to see a silent shadow flapping through the trees with a tasty morsel for him. But all he heard was the snapping and crackling of branches under their icy burdens. The only thing moving was a red fox slipping gracefully along a trail.

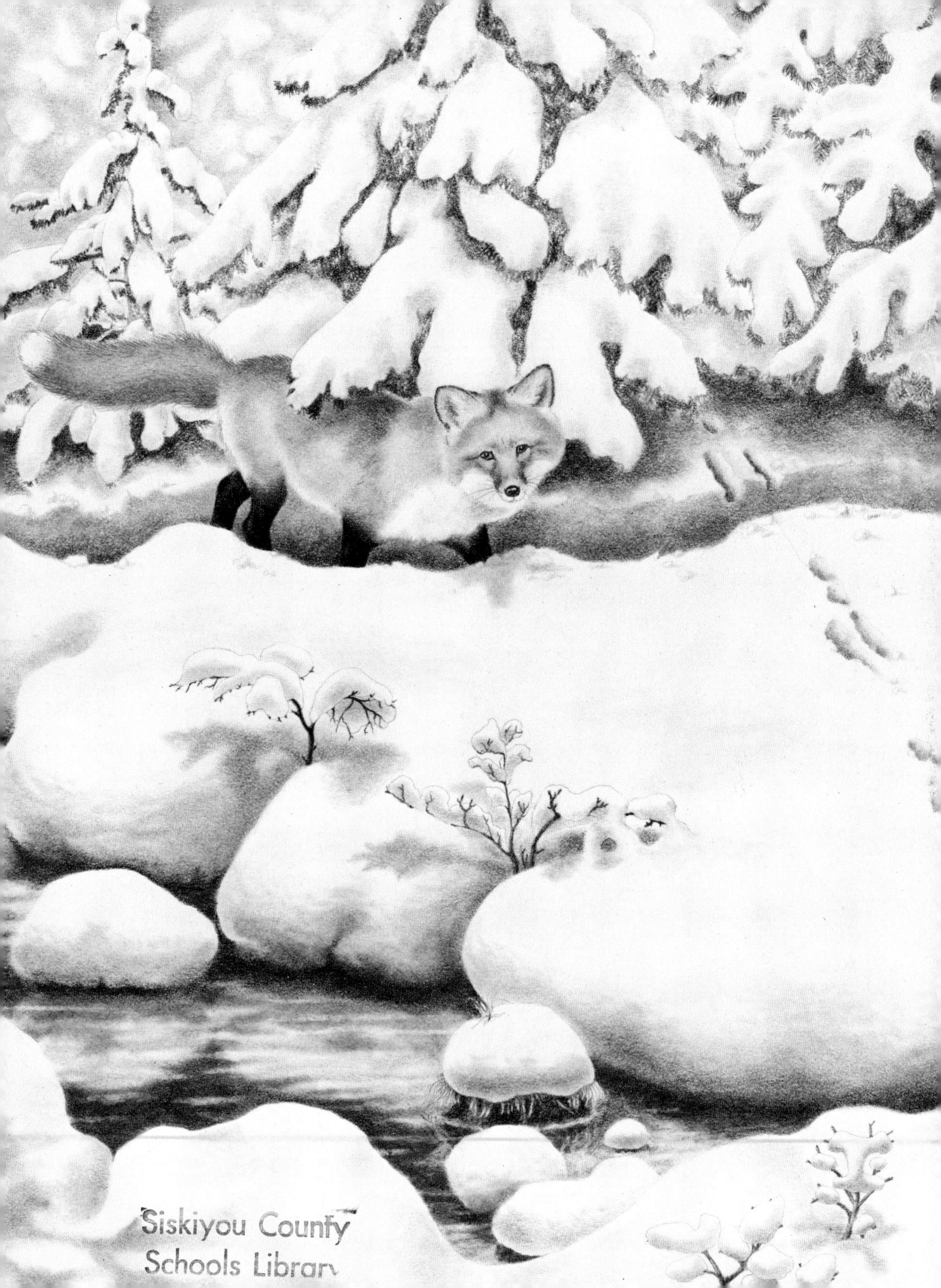

When he looked for familiar trees and landmarks, he found nothing he had ever seen before. Calling and crying, he flew deeper and deeper into the strange woods searching for his parents, but he never saw them again.

So Owlet was now on his own. Some days he went hungry, but he became a better hunter as the winter weeks passed, and soon he was catching rabbits and skunks as well as his parents could have. The strange forest soon seemed like home to him. As he flew through it night after night, a part of it became his very own.

An old tree covered with vine maple became his favorite sleeping roost, and it was soon splattered with his droppings and pellets.

Another tree nearby was his eating roost, and over the weeks it became decorated with mouse tails, feathers, rabbit feet, and other leftovers.

The summer that followed was a very hot one. Many times Owlet perched limply in his sleeping-roost tree all day long and dangled his wings to cool off his sides. As the hot days dragged by, he spent a lot of time miserably panting, with his eyes closed and his beak wide open. But the nights were cool in the woods, and because he was a good hunter he grew to be a strong and healthy owl.

When autumn rolled around, Owlet was restless and lonely.

Sometimes he sat on his roost and tried out the new voice he was getting.

"Wha-ah-ah!" he cried, but it didn't sound just right, so he tried some other sounds. In a deep hollow voice he hooted, "Oh-o-o-o!" "Oooooooooooo-hu-hu-hoooooo!" he tried. Then, "Who-hoo-hoo!" He repeated that one several times. It felt *almost* right to him. Finally he made a call that seemed perfect: "Whoo, whoo, hu-whoo! Whoo, whoo, hu-whoo, ah!" Sure enough, it was the usual call of the Great Horned Owl.

All owls learn their calls through trial and error, experiment and practice. The Great Horned Owl makes other sounds, too, such as growls, rasping barks, and crazy laughter for reasons only owls know. But it always returns to "Whoo, hoooo, hoooooo!" and "Whoo-hoooo, who-hoooo, hoooo!" even if it was born in captivity and has never heard another Great Horned Owl hooting.

Owlet often cried this lonesome sound out into the empty woods. One winter night, someone answered back — a soft, high sound, "Hoo, hooo, hoooo! Hoo-hooo, hoo-hoooo, hoo!" from far away. For a moment Owlet stood perfectly still on the dark branch, his eyes getting bigger and bigger. Then he hooted excitedly, jumped off his roost, and glided toward the distant hoots.

"Whoo, whoo, hu-whoo!" he cried as he flew.

"Hoo, hoo, hu-whoo, ah!" the voice answered from a bushy spruce. Suddenly Owlet saw the other owl. She stood shyly on a branch of the spruce, watching him with big sunflower-yellow eyes. He lit in an oak tree several feet away and stared at her. He moved his head up and down, from side to side, and finally tilted it all the way over sideways to see her better.

"Whooo," said Owlet, not certain what to do next.

"Hooo," she replied softly.

Owlet leaped off his branch and flew to a limb just in front of her. He bobbed and bowed his head, clicked his beak softly,

then ruffled and flattened his feathers as she watched. Then he jumped to a place beside her on her branch and dipped his head, drooped his wings, and lifted his tail feathers to the sky. His throat swelled out and a strange voice came from him — a voice he'd never used before. Deep and booming, it cried, "HOO-HOO-WHOO-WHOO-HOOOO-HOOOO!" Then Owlet stood back up straight and peeked at her.

Bowing gracefully, she did exactly what he had done, in her softer, higher, faster voice. Owlet was almost bouncing on the limb with excitement! Here, at last, was someone to share his sleeping roost and eating roost! They rubbed their beaks together

contentedly. All night long they bowed and dipped and hooted and clicked and rubbed beaks. When dawn started to creep into the sky, Owlet glided off the branch and wheeled slowly, waiting for her to follow. They flew soundlessly, hungry but contented, to his roost.

The winter was kind to Owlet and his mate, and they flew and hunted together in the snowy forest. One day in February, she started looking for a nest. She lit in every tree that seemed right and poked her head into old squirrel nests, hollow trees, hawk nests, and crow nests. She finally picked a hollow tree that stood all alone in a clearing. Then she looked around until she found a good sleeping roost nearby, within sight of the nest tree. Thereafter, they always came back to the new sleeping roost after a night of hunting.

The hollow tree seemed to be special to Owlet's mate. She never brought sticks or feathers to line it, because Great Horned Owls don't do that. But she spent a lot of time going in and out the doorway and sitting in the nest's hollow middle. Owlet seldom sat on the nest. He perched on the roost tree when he wasn't hunting and he sometimes lit on a branch of the hollow tree when his mate was sitting inside. Almost all of the brooding would be done by his mate, and Owlet's job would be to feed her as she sat there.

One night a few weeks after Owlet's mate had chosen her nesting tree, the two owls were hunting together. Suddenly she turned in midair and started back through the woods toward her nest. Like a dark arrow she streaked, with a puzzled Owlet following behind her. What was happening? Into the door hole she bounced, making a quick turn-around in the nest, and suddenly, with a soft *plop,* there was the egg! She rolled it quickly under her warm breast feathers with her feathered toes, peeked out the doorway at the anxious Owlet, then settled down for the long wait through the cold winter weeks. And Owlet knew what had happened. He leaped off the limb where he had been watching and glided silently into the night to get a snack for his mate.